A First-Start Easy Reader

This easy reader contains only 45 different words,
repeated often to help the young reader develop
word recognition and interest in reading.

Basic word list for *Easter Bunny's Lost Egg*

it	here	last
is	egg	Easter
the	eggs	Bunny
has	and	comes
a	says	basket
he	will	painted
of	hide	where
in	one	think
his	five	under
hop	that	porch
are	now	rock
let	did	bush
me	hid	flower
I	but	tree
my	sit	oops

Easter Bunny's Lost Egg

Written by Sharon Gordon

Illustrated by John Magine

Troll Associates

ISBN 0-89375-275-4

Hop! Hop! Hop!

It is the Easter Bunny.

Here comes the Easter Bunny.

The Easter Bunny has a basket.

He has a basket of eggs.

In his basket are five eggs.

He has five painted eggs.

"Let me think," says the Easter Bunny.

"Where will I hide my eggs?"

"Where will I hide

my five painted eggs?"

"I will hide one under the porch."

"I will hide one under the rock."

"I will hide one under the bush."

"I will hide one under the flower."

"And I will hide one
under the tree."

"Now let me think," says the Easter Bunny.

"Where did I hide

my five painted eggs?"

"I hid one under the porch."

"I hid one under the rock."

"I hid one under the bush."

"I hid one under the flower."

"But where did I hide
my last painted egg?
Let me think,"
says the Easter Bunny.

"I will sit and think
under the tree."

"Oops," says the Easter Bunny.

"That is where I hid

my last painted egg!"

Hop! Hop! Hop!